THE
SECRET
OF THE
TARA BELLE

One Boy's Quest for Truth About the Father He Lost

SUSAN MASON

SILVERSMITH
PRESS

Published by Silversmith Press–Houston, Texas
www.silversmithpress.com

ISBN 978-1-961093-59-1 (Softcover Book)
ISBN 978-1-961093-60-7 (eBook)

CONTENTS

Chapter One 5

Chapter Two..11

Chapter Three 16

Chapter Four..18

Chapter Five..25

Chapter Six 28

Chapter Seven 32

Chapter Eight..37

Chapter Nine 40

Chapter Ten..44

Chapter Eleven..48

Chapter Twelve..53

Chapter Thirteen..56

Chapter Fourteen..62

Chapter Fifteen 65

Chapter Sixteen..69

Chapter Seventeen 73

Chapter Eighteen 81

Chapter Nineteen..86

CHAPTER ONE

Out of the gloom stared the painted almond eyes. Unseeing, they gazed from a flawless golden countenance, crowned by an elaborate headdress striped blue and gold.

Dan surveyed the mask. *Awesome,* he thought. One could truly believe this was the face of a god. He bent forward to get a closer look, his dark, curly hair falling forward over his tanned face.

And the Egyptians really believed such a mask bore a pharaoh into the afterlife, he mused. He tried to imagine the scene as ancient goddesses cast their magical spells of protection over this young king's lifeless body, over his divine skin of gold and bones of silver...

Dan couldn't help but jump when someone touched him on the shoulder.

"Cool, isn't it?"

His friend Peter was standing behind him in the gloom.

"Quite spooky, really, all these ancient treasures lit up, surrounded by pitch-darkness," Dan said. "I suppose it was a bit like that when they found them in the tomb."

Peter looked around. Each museum exhibit had been illuminated with great care. Jewel-like enamel colors gleamed, and gold shone from delicate ornaments, ornate dishes, masks, even furniture.

"Wasn't there a curse of the mummies, or something?" he asked.

"Yeah, legend has it, there's an ancient curse on the tombs of the Egyptian pharaohs. Disturbing the embalmed remains is said to bring bad luck. And there may be something to that. Not long after Tutankhamun's tomb was discovered, the man who bank-rolled the whole expedition was found dead of blood poisoning. And someone who took artifacts from the tomb back to England had his house burn down. Stuff like that."

"Cool," said Peter. "Looking around at a bunch of dusty old relics isn't so bad after all. But I'm still glad you could make it today, mate. It's made having to bring my sister here to the museum a bit more bearable."

"No problem. After all, there's not much to do in Moorton-on-Sea on a rainy day in the summer holidays. By the look of how busy it is in here, quite a few people had the same idea. The World War II room wasn't so great, but these Egyptian replicas are okay."

"Yeah, and I just read over there, the pharaohs sometimes married their sisters. Can you imagine?" said Peter.

"Ooh, yuck! Sounds awful," came a disembodied voice. Naomi appeared out of the shadows. It was easy to see she was Peter's sister. She had the same fair complexion with the odd freckle, and the same auburn hair. "Can't think of anything worse," she said cheekily.

"Likewise," said Peter.

"This place is like Indiana Jones finding the lost treasure," she said, gazing at one of the glass cases. "Look at this casket!"

A moment later she said, "Did you see in the next room, there's a huge dinosaur?"

"No, really? I don't remember reading anything about dino-saurs when we came in. That's a result. Want to check it out, Dan?"

"Sure."

"Okay, it's this way," said Naomi.

They all blinked as they came out into the light again. They were in a high-ceilinged hall, bordered by skylights. Around the walls were displayed replicas of various extinct species. Dominating the centre of the room was a huge model of a Tyrannosaurus Rex.

"Wow, I knew the T-Rex was big, but is that really life-size?' marvelled Dan. "It's massive."

"Wouldn't want to come across one of them on a dark night," joked Peter.

"Don't be silly, you couldn't meet one of those. They've been extinct for millions of years," his sister corrected him.

"Millions? I'm sure it's billions!"

"Well, actually, it's gazillions!" she giggled.

They spread out to have a look at the exhibits.

Reading details of the Dodo, Dan gasped.

"Hey, listen to this. The name Dodo probably relates to the Dutch word Dodaars, which means either 'fat-arse' or 'knot-arse'! Hilarious!" he laughed.

"Fat-arse! You're kidding me! Let me have a look at that."

Peter came over and the two of them laughed heartily.

Meanwhile, Naomi had come across a model of a skeleton.

"That's a plesiosaur," said the museum guide, a young man who was standing close by.

"Is that so? I don't think I've ever heard of one of those before."

"Yes, you can see it here in the pictures. It was a large, marine reptile of the Early Jurassic period."

"Really? A sea-going dinosaur?"

Naomi looked at the small head, the long, slender neck, the broad turtle-like body, short tail and two pairs of large, elongated flippers extending from its body.

"It doesn't look like it would be much good underwater."

"You're right, it doesn't seem to have the most streamlined of forms. But you might be surprised. Those paddles would be extremely strong. They could probably move gallons of water with one pass."

By now, the boys had joined them. With a growing audience, the guide started to gather momentum.

"Most people don't know that the first complete skeleton of a plesiosaur was discovered by Mary Anning, an early palaeontologist and fossil hunter, right here in England."

"That's cool," said Peter. "To have something here, I mean. Exciting things always seem to happen thousands of miles away, in other countries."

"Well, England was the site of many plesiosaur fossil finds in the nineteenth century, especially in the quarries of Dorset."

"Wow, that close? Peter, we should go and check them out," said Dan.

"Well, if you're looking for proximity, we here in Moorton have our own claim to fame. Did you know," the guide now leaned in and lowered his voice, "we had our own discovery of a modern-day dinosaur right here in Moorton?"

Naomi gasped. "No, how is that possible? They're extinct!"

"It caused quite a stir, I remember. I was still at school when it happened." The guide was clearly enjoying telling the story.

"There was this fishing trawler operating off the coast here, when it brought up this strange carcass in its net. The captain wanted to throw it back overboard immediately, as he was concerned it would contaminate the whole catch, but there was a marine biologist on board…"

There was a marine biologist on board. Dan's heart missed a beat at the guide's words. He didn't hear what was said after that. Darkness descended around him. He felt like he was no longer standing in the museum hall.

"My father was a marine biologist," he said quietly in the dark.

"Well, what a coincidence," he heard the guide say enthusiastically.

"You would probably understand a lot of this from your dad, then. Anyway, as I was saying…"

Dan still couldn't see anything. He wondered what was happening. Then gradually the darkness cleared, and he found himself standing outside, surrounded by plants and flowers bathed in dazzling sunshine. He was in some sort of park or garden. Not far away he could make out two shapes. As they moved around, he realised they were people. One figure came towards him. It loomed tall over him as it drew closer. Then it must have bent down, for a face appeared, close to his.

Dark tousled curls fell forward over a tanned, smiling face. The expression was warm, generous, and playful. Dan saw the lips move, but he couldn't hear what was being said. Then that smile again, with a light that shone from those eyes that was like the light of life itself.

Dan realised he was reliving a moment from his early childhood. He was gazing into the face of the father he'd lost many years ago. All memories of that time had been locked away, unrecollected, until this moment.

As Dan looked up into that face, he instinctively knew this person smiling down would do absolutely anything for him. He could hardly breathe, so overwhelming was the sense of comfort and acceptance that wrapped itself around him. It felt like being set adrift, cradled upon a gentle breeze of unseen, loving arms, a place of utter peace and complete wholeness. Right there, Dan felt he lacked absolutely nothing. He could have stayed there forever, gazing up into that shining countenance.

But the perfect tranquillity began to fracture as slowly, to Dan's dismay, the image began to fade. Alarmed, he wondered how he could hold onto this moment, this vision. He was struck by an overwhelming sense of longing as it disappeared. *Don't go!* he thought, in distress.

From somewhere close by he heard Peter's voice.

"Are you alright, Dan? You look like you've seen a ghost."

Dan's vision cleared. He looked at Peter and said, "I need to get out of here."

His friend could see there was something very wrong.

"Okay, let's go."

Naomi began to protest.

"We'll come back another time, Sis, don't worry."

They hastily thanked the guide for his time and left.

CHAPTER TWO

Dan gazed down at the welcome mug of piping hot chocolate he cradled in his hands. Peter stirred his mug while Naomi toyed with her steaming plate of chips.

"Sorry to bring things to such an abrupt end, Naomi," said Dan. "I just had to get out of there."

It felt comforting to be in the café, as he looked outside at the rain still pouring over the road, the deserted promenade, and the frothing sea beyond.

"What happened?" asked Peter. "You were so pale. You looked like you'd seen a ghost."

Dan sighed to himself. *Yes, I suppose I have*, he thought.

"It was when that guide started talking. I had like a flash-back. I remembered something I've never recalled before. I saw my dad."

He paused. "I suppose it's my earliest memory."

"Your dad was lost at sea, wasn't he? What happened, if it's okay to ask?"

"It's okay. The truth is, I don't know. Mum never seemed very keen to talk about it."

Dan took a sip from his mug.

"I don't remember my dad. Well, I didn't until now. And I didn't think about him very much when I was young. I suppose that was because it has always been just me and Mum. You know, when something has always been that way. When I might have tried to ask more about him well, that's when Mum got sick. And then the Dragon came, after that."

Peter nodded. He knew who Dan meant. Dan didn't get on with his grandmother.

"But why did you start thinking about these things in the museum? The guide was talking about the carcass catch."

"It was when he mentioned the marine biologist. It's like I just knew he was talking about my father."

"Is that possible? Could that really have been your dad?"

"To be honest, I don't know. I didn't hear much else after that."

Suddenly the café door burst open, and a noisy group of teenage boys came in. Dan looked up, and then turned away.

"Don't look now," he said under his breath, "but it's Chesterton's lot."

Peter hunched over his mug, eyes on the table.

"What's your soup of the day?" a weasel-like boy asked the woman behind the counter.

Out of the corner of his eye, Dan could see that while the waitress was occupied, a thuggish-looking boy was helping himself to cookies from a jar at the other end of the counter. The other two were leaning in front of him, making it as hard as possible for anyone to see what he was doing.

Dan knew it would be pointless to call them out. They would just lie their heads off. Did they really have nothing better to do? It wasn't like Chesterton was short of money.

Surely, he'll just take what he wants and leave, thought Dan.

After a further brief interchange with the waitress, it looked like the decoy's job was done. The lid was back on the cookie jar.

"Chesterton, please leave, please leave," Dan said under his breath.

But the thief had caught sight of them and sauntered over to their table.

"Well, well, Murray and Jenkins. Fancy meeting you here. What's that on your plate, missy? Chips? Let us have some."

He leant over the table and took a handful.

Naomi was about to say something but got a swift kick from her brother under the table.

"Mmm, nice," said the boy, as the other three came over. "Needs more salt, though."

"Alright, Peter?" said the decoy.

"Alright, Matt," responded Peter, uneasily.

"We're going to the skate park this weekend, if you want to come."

The ringleader looked annoyed at this invitation, but then smiled and said, "Yes, come on down to the skate park. We're one big happy family down there. I'm sure you'd love it!"

Matt, emboldened and obviously missing the clear sarcasm in this comment, said, "It's open from 7:00 p.m. and…" A clip around the ear cut him short.

"That's enough chit chat," retorted Chesterton, "unless you want my dad to give your dad the boot."

Matt looked genuinely alarmed.

Chesterton laughed cruelly as he turned away.

"Just kidding. Come on, boys. Time to leave."

The wind whipped momentarily through the open door, and then they were gone. Peter gave a sigh of relief.

"Thank goodness for that. Are you alright Sis? Got any chips left?"

"Not many," said Naomi, forlornly.

"Don't worry. We'll get you some more."

They went up to the counter to order.

Dan shook his head. *Neanderthal*, he thought. He was fuming.

Who does he think he is? Pushing everyone around, acting like he owns the place. But then again, Chesterton Fisheries was the biggest fishing business in the region. In a way, the Chestertons did own the place. Dan felt sick at the thought.

In an attempt to shake off his annoyance, Dan turned his mind back to what had happened at the museum. Now that time had distanced him from the incident, he truly started to question whether he had overreacted. Maybe it was just a coincidence. Maybe anyone's mention of a marine biologist would have triggered that memory from his childhood. He had to find out.

Peter and Naomi returned with another plate of chips.

"We've got doughnuts, too," beamed Naomi. The prospect apparently had a miraculous effect, dispersing the clouds that had gathered over her sunny disposition.

"Excellent," said Dan, giving Peter a knowing look. "I knew we were missing something."

"Yep, it's all good," said Peter. "Let's forget about those idiots. They're a bunch of losers, anyway."

As they settled back down at the table, Dan attempted to resume their conversation.

"Peter, I need to know more about what that guide at the museum said. Can you remember anything else?"

"Well," said Peter, "where were we?"

"The fishing boat caught a plesiosaur carcass," said Naomi, helpfully.

"Oh yes. Well, the guide said something about how the biologist persuaded the captain to keep the carcass on board so he could at least record all its details. So, he took measurements, diagrams, photos, you know, that sort of thing."

Dan's heart leapt. Could it have been his father on board, examining the carcass?

"Everyone thought they had found a modern-day dinosaur,

though," Peter continued. "Moorton was on the map, in all the news. International TV and everything. Quite famous really, for a while."

Peter looked at Dan's face. It had an odd expression.

"That's what the guide said, anyway," Peter said, almost apologetically.

They sat in silence for a while. *Could this really be my father?* Dan wondered.

Suddenly Dan realised, there was an easy way he could tell if it wasn't the case.

"When did this all happen?' he asked.

"Oh, I don't know. I think it was about ten or twelve years ago, the guide said. Can you remember, Sis?"

"Yes," she said, "He said it was about twelve years ago."

The timing could fit. And somehow Dan knew it was him.

CHAPTER THREE

It was a long bike ride to Lymchester Hospital. His grandmother drove there, whenever she visited, but Dan preferred to go to see his mum by himself. He stopped at the ward station to check with the nurses where his mum was this time and then made his way to Room 11. The vertical blinds were almost completely closed against the mid-day light, but Dan could still make out the form that lay under the blankets in the bed. He drew closer. He could hear shallow, regular breathing. Right beside the bed, now, he gazed down at the pale, sleeping countenance, the hair greying before its time.

"Hello, Mum," he whispered. "It's Dan. How're you doing today?"

There was no answer. He hadn't expected one. He sat down on the bedside chair and leaned forward, close to his mother's face.

"I had quite a day, yesterday," he whispered. "Peter had to take his sister to the museum, so he asked me to come too. It was quite a laugh."

Dan fidgeted with the edge of the blanket. His expression changed.

"There was something else, though. I found out about how the year Dad died there'd been a marine biologist on a fishing trawler that caught a strange carcass–possibly a plesiosaur. I know you don't like talking about those sorts of things, but I was wondering, well…if it was Dad."

No answer. The shallow breathing continued its steady rhythm.

Dan sighed and hung his head. He guessed he was on his own again for this one. It seemed a lifetime ago that he had lived with his mum in simple, contented, daily routines. Their uncomplicated life together had been sweet; how he'd taken it for granted. He mourned their intimacy lost.

If he could have turned the clock back, there was one thing he would definitely have changed. He would have asked her more about his father. Dan regretted how he had never done so when he had had the chance. He felt a pang of remorse. Was he heartless? Guilty of not caring about his own father? But the truth is, he'd not wanted to cause his mother the pain he'd clearly sensed, whenever their talk got too close to this subject.

Dan leaned forward again, whispering, "Come back, Mum. Come back."

Time passed, unaccounted for, save for the light below the blinds that moved across the floor and the sound of his mother's shallow breathing.

It was sometime later when Dan finally rose and gently straightened the blankets around his mother's form.

He quietly made his way out, closing the door behind him with a click.

CHAPTER FOUR

It was late in the day when Dan got home. Having opened the front door quietly, he lifted his bike into the hall and leant it up against the wall.

He could hear the TV. A gameshow presenter was making some corny joke at the expense of a contestant. Prompted laughter and then applause. Now the all-important question about something that no-one in real life cared about. The contestant was deliberating. Dan found it nauseating.

He edged forward just enough to see into the living room. There was the usual tea tray: teapot shrouded with a home-made knitted tea-cosy, cup and saucer, chipped milk jug, and a plate of sad biscuits. Dan did the best he could to not make a sound as he passed the doorway. He headed up the stairs, careful to avoid the third step, which creaked.

Dan turned on the desk lamp. The rest of his room was in shadow. It was simply furnished. A bookcase housed a small collection of books, including a handful of novels, several art books, and some scientific and medical reference works. There was a cluster of paint brushes in a jar on the top shelf.

A small, framed photo of a much younger Dan with his mum,

in happier times, was on the bedside cabinet. Some paintings and charcoal drawings were displayed around the walls, landscapes and still life, and still others were on the floor, unframed, leaning up against the wall. A wardrobe and chest of drawers were the only other items apart from the desk where he sat.

Dan turned on his computer. Finding out about his dad was now foremost in his mind. The time had come to face his history, his provenance.

Let's ask the one who knows everything, he said to himself. He opened up the browser and paused. What should he search? It was strange to be googling his own father, but that seemed the best place to start.

William Jenkins, he typed. Dan knew he'd been known by his friends and family as Will. That's what his mother had always called him, the few times she'd mentioned him to others in his hearing. But Dan thought the full name might bring up better search results.

The listing came up on the screen. Dan scrolled through it. A myriad of William Jenkins, spanning history from all over the world, were listed. That wasn't any good. Obviously far too general.

William Jenkins marine biologist would be better, he thought.

Apparently, there was an eminent Dr. William Jenkins who was a marine biologist in Canada. Lots of references about him. Another biologist called William Jenkins had lived in Australia. Dan scrolled further down the page, searching for anything promising. It looked like he needed to get still more specific if he didn't want to be clicking through pages and pages of this stuff.

The cursor blinked in the search bar. He knew what he needed to type. He took a deep breath.

Death of William Jenkins marine biologist Moorton.

Dan looked at what he'd typed.

He felt a sudden dull ache, deep inside. He'd never really allowed himself to feel the loss of his father before. It had been pushed away, deep under the practicalities of his life, like something covered in the folds of a heavy garment. Muffled, smothered. But now he realised that all these years it had always cast a shadow over his life.

Resolutely, he hit *Enter.*

He found a notice in the local paper, *Moorton News,* that read simply:

JENKINS, William Daniel, of Moorton, formerly of Newcastle, passed away on Wednesday, 25th August 1999. Beloved husband of Sarah Eleanor Jenkins, dearly loved father of Daniel and loved brother of Robert. Will be sadly missed by his family and many dear friends. Aged 35 years. Remembered with love. Relatives and friends are invited to attend William's memorial service to be held at Christ Church, 5 High Street, Moorton on....

Dan re-read the sad little notice. So commonplace, so matter of fact. It sounded like it should be about someone else's dad. But maybe not so commonplace. *Aged 35 years.* That was an untimely death. Not a life that ended naturally, full of decades of experiences and memories. Not a life full of years.

Dan sighed. Leaning forward, he searched for anything that might yield more about William Jenkins' death. There was a press release in the *Moorton News* which read:

Tragic Death of Local Man, 35, Killed on Wednesday

A young man from Moorton lost his life in a tragic accident on a fishing trawler on Wednesday.

William Jenkins, who was aged 35, described by friends as a "generous and talented" person, sadly died last Wednesday evening.

William, who was from Moorton, died as the result of a tragic accident on board the fishing trawler, Tara Belle.

Police were notified by HM coastguard of a mayday call being received from a vessel at about 20:40 BST on the evening in question. The boat was located 30 miles offshore when the incident occurred.

The Bureau of Marine Accident Investigation (BMAI) are still investigating the circumstances which led to William Jenkins' death and are receiving full co-operation from the boat's crew and the trawler owners, Chesterton Fisheries.

Tributes have been made to William by devastated friends and colleagues who have said the 35-year-old had been "outgoing and kind-hearted" with "an amazing scientific mind," and "a promising career cut short."

So, his father had died in some sort of accident on a trawler called *Tara Belle*. But what, exactly? Presumably he had been working on the boat, although his mum had never said he was a fisherman. Maybe he had been working in some sort of scientific capacity? Was it the same trawler that had brought the carcass up in its nets? No mention of that.

Plesiosaur carcass Moorton, typed Dan. The screen filled with headlines again:

Sea-Monster or Shark: An Alleged Plesiosaur Carcass; English Fishing Boat Catches Sea Monster; Body of Prehistoric Marine Animal Found…

Dan clicked on a heading and started to read:

Whilst fishing for mackerel, the English trawler Tara Belle, from the fishery company, Chesterton Fisheries, brought up a decomposing carcass in its nets. The catch came up from a depth of about 1000 feet. The 15-strong crew offered differing opinions of what the beast might be. Some thought it was a rotting whale, while others suggested it may be a sea turtle which was missing its shell.

The crew agreed that the carcass should be examined and photographed. William Jenkins (a marine science graduate who was on board), measured the animal which had an overall length of about 10 feet. He also took some horny fibre samples from an anterior fin and several photographs. He made sketches of the creature, and a considerable number of observational notes. Jenkins concluded, on the basis of his findings, that the specimen was not a fish, but was possibly a juvenile, plesiosaur-like animal that had never been documented before. Tragically, Jenkins was killed in an accident on board the Tara Belle not long after he worked on his analysis of the carcass.

Upon the boat's return, Jenkins' records became the focus of claims that the carcass (which had somehow disappeared from the container in which it had been stored) may indeed have been that of a long extinct plesiosaur, a type of small-headed, long necked marine reptile. If this was so, the find would confirm these dinosaurs of the sea are not, as thought, lost to the world.

Monster fever gripped Moorton and the rest of the nation. An entire advertising campaign was produced on sea monsters by the company that had made the camera used to photograph the find. Toy manufacturers put plushies of the plesiosaur into production.

Meanwhile, researchers and experts studied the evidence. Eventually they published their report. It was determined that the mystery find was nothing more than a shark, probably a young basking shark. These creatures have been known to decay in a manner that makes them resemble the form of a plesiosaur.

Dan sat back in his chair. So, the *Tara Belle* had been the setting for both the carcass discovery and his father's demise. It was rather odd that there was no more information about how his father had died. And it looked like the carcass had been misidentified. Strange that the remains had gone missing, so all that was left were the records made on the boat.

He ran his eye down the page. Headlines indicated further articles discrediting the discovery. When he checked a few out, it was clear they were all quoting from the same report:

Initial chromatography tests showed a profile of amino acids closely resembling a control sample from a blue shark… fin rays were observed, which are possessed by most fish, including sharks… the bony phalanges which served as flipper supports on a plesiosaur were not seen on the carcass… one of the photos showed an apparent dorsal fin, present in most fish, including sharks, but not known to have occurred in plesiosaurs…

Dan was no marine expert. In fact, he steered clear of anything marine-related. But the evidence seemed conclusive. His heart sank. The dull ache gave way to outright pain. This was the last piece of work his father had produced. It was his final legacy. And it seemed to have been erroneous. Somehow that made the events that followed the discovery all the more painful for Dan. He wanted to cry, but no tears came.

He slowly finished scrolling to the bottom of the page. All the headlines seemed to say the same thing, some of them even using the same phrases. He was just about to close the tab when his eye caught the very last headline, *The Tara Belle Cryptid: Questioning the Official View.*

Opening the page, Dan's eyes fell on the summary:

Jenkins felt the flippers, which were still reasonably intact, and was able to discern hard, bone-like material, like the five phalanges expected in

*a mammal's flipper, rather than the cartilaginous fin rays of a shark...
that the horny fibres had a similar amino acid composition is far from
being a crucial means of identification. Besides, the samples came from
different parts of the respective specimens... Jenkins' (and the crew's)
first-hand identification of a flipper was summarily dismissed by the
"experts" and reclassified as a dorsal fin, albeit of an "unnatural
appearance," precluding the carcass from being that of a mammal...*

Dan was surprised, and pleased, to discover there was someone who had an alternative take on the evidence, even if they
appeared to be vastly outnumbered. The pain inside eased a little.
Maybe his father hadn't made the errors in his investigation that
the researchers and experts asserted after all.

Dan turned off the computer, leaned on the desk and rested
his head in his hands. He could hardly get his head around all that
had happened over the last two days, and he suddenly felt terribly
tired. Whatever he thought, or whatever he would do, about what
he had learnt, would have to wait until tomorrow. He switched
the lamp off and fell, fully clothed, onto his bed. Within moments
he was asleep.

CHAPTER FIVE

When Dan woke up, the light diffusing through the curtains suggested the sun had been up for some time.

It must be late, he thought. He rolled over and checked the clock. Yep, it was late alright. 11:30 a.m.

"Time to rise and shine," he grimaced to himself, and sat up, stiffly. *Crashing out in your clothes isn't the most comfortable way to get some sleep,* Dan thought. Time for a shower.

As Dan came down the stairs, he could smell something good cooking. He had conflicting feelings. Eggs and bacon would be most welcome right now, but then…

He entered the kitchen. Some bedraggled flowers drooped in a vase. A puzzle booklet lay open at a half-finished crossword on the check-covered table set for two. At the stove, back turned, was a stout, aproned woman with grey, curly hair, serving up from the sizzling frying pan.

"Morning, Gran," said Dan.

"Good afternoon to you, young man," said his grandmother, over her shoulder. "I heard you in the shower, so I thought I'd make us some breakfast, now you're up."

"That's great. Thanks Gran," said Dan, but he knew it was an uncharacteristic gesture. He often had to fend for himself in the kitchen. He couldn't help wondering what Gran wanted.

"Well now, here we are," said Gran, turning around with a plate in each hand. Dan drew up his chair as she put them down on the table.

"It looks like the rain has cleared for the time-being, which is a mercy. What are you planning to do today, young man?"

Dan wasn't about to share his plans with his grandmother. For the most part, they kept out of each other's way. Fortunately, Gran didn't wait long for an answer before continuing.

"I'm going to Lymchester today to see my friend Janice and do a bit of shopping. I'm not sure what time I'll be back. There's some ham in the fridge and a bit of salad left over, if you're wanting a sandwich later."

"Okay Gran."

They ate in silence for a while.

"You know the hospital's keeping your mum in for tests after her recent episode?" she said, eyes focused on her plate.

"Of course."

"You went to see her yesterday, didn't you?"

Dan put his knife and fork down.

"So?"

"Well, I just wanted to remind you that your Mum's health is in a very delicate state at the moment. She's been absolutely exhausted recently. The doctors have advised that visits or any other disturbance could be extremely detrimental."

Dan couldn't believe his ears.

"Visits? From her own son?" he seethed.

"I'm just trying to give your mum the best chance of recovery."

"I bet you are!"

Dan stood up.

"You don't need to remind me what sort of problems people

with MS have. I probably know more about it than you do. And Mum wasn't "disturbed" by my visit, for your information. As for the doctors, they can keep doing their wretched tests if they want. But it seems to me, she's just keeps getting worse."

He stormed down the hall and grabbed his bike and pack.

"I'll see Mum when I want to!" he shouted as he went out, slamming the door behind him.

CHAPTER SIX

Dan was still fuming as he cycled through the town. He didn't notice the busy traffic on the familiar narrow streets. Without registering, he dodged the hazardous tourists spilling off the pavement into his path. He didn't even notice his favourite building as he passed it; a Georgian construction housing the region's renowned art collection.

He made his way to the beach and then cycled east along the coast, away from the quay, with its tourist noise, amusements, and pleasure boats; docks for trawlers and other mercantile vessels were out of sight, beyond West Head.

Cycling along the coast road had a soothing effect on him. The sea breeze seemed to blow through his angst, cooling, calming, cleansing the churning inside. He embraced the fresh, cool sensation that enveloped his whole body. Things weren't looking so bad.

Eventually he arrived at a pontoon. A small sailing boat was drawn up alongside. Two individuals were busy making it secure. As Dan drew closer, he could see it was two youngsters, a boy and a girl. The girl turned and waved, calling something out. He couldn't hear what she said.

Dan leant his bike against the shed at the end of the pontoon and walked up to meet them.

"I thought I'd miss you today," he said.

"The wind picked up quite a bit," said Peter, "so we took longer to get back in. It was fun hiking, though."

"We got the spinnaker up for a run, too," said Naomi.

Then came Dan and Peter's familiar ritual.

"Want to come out for a spin?"

"No, thanks. Maybe next time."

It was always the same. Although Dan loved the sea in many ways, he couldn't quite bring himself to board a vessel. The sea was beautiful, bountiful, strong, but also dangerous, treacherous, containing many deep secrets. And the sea was custodian of his father and his story, and it wasn't yielding anything.

"I'm starving," said Peter, as he stripped off his gloves. "It must be cod and chips time."

"Yeah," said Naomi, "I can't wait."

Once all their equipment was put in the shed, the three of them headed towards the delicious smell of fried onions coming from the nearby kiosk.

Sitting on the beach, Peter and Naomi consumed their lunch with relish.

"Don't feed the gulls," said Dan, eyeing the birds hovering and periodically swooping close by, "You'll never get rid of them."

He paused. Should he tell them what he had discovered in his research last night? He decided he would.

"You know that plesiosaur story we found out about at the museum? The one I thought my father had something to do with? Well, I did some digging last night."

He proceeded to tell them what he had found out had happened on the *Tara Belle*.

"That's quite a story," said Peter. He hesitated. "Are you okay talking about this stuff? It can't be easy."

"I'm okay," said Dan. Upon reflection he said, "It helps to talk about it, actually."

"Did the papers really not give any details about your dad's accident?' asked Peter. "That seems odd. How do you feel about that? If my dad died, I'd sure want to know what happened."

"Yes, I want to find out the whole story—what happened. But things got even stranger once the boat came back to port."

He then told them about the frenzied media interest, the disappearance of the carcass and the experts' verdict in their published report.

"That's disappointing that it seems to have been a misidentification. It would have been so cool. But how strange that the carcass was 'lost,'" Peter said with air quotes. "Sounds a bit dodgy to me."

"Yeah, how likely is that? That you'd mislay a potentially significant specimen of such scientific, even prehistoric, importance? It doesn't make sense. Someone must know something."

Dan picked up a pebble and looked at it for a moment, before throwing it as far as he could. It landed in the sea with a plop.

"It's a real mystery!" piped up Naomi.

Dan didn't appreciate this statement of the obvious from Peter's know-it-all little sister. He would have preferred it if she hadn't been there to hear their conversation. He wasn't sure how much she could keep to herself.

"Yeah, and it's a mystery we're not likely to solve," said Dan despondently.

Peter looked uncomfortable as he crushed up his lunch wrappings and looked around for a bin.

"Sorry mate. I know it's not the best news to be finding out."

His face suddenly brightened.

"But look on the bright side. At least you're not in a state like old Whiskey Wainwright down there."

Peter gestured towards West Head, the other end of the bay. Dan knew who he meant. It was too far to see, but he could picture the ramshackle building that served as a home for the old fisherman everyone knew by that name.

"Hey," said Peter, leaning forward and punching Dan in the arm, "Do you remember when we paid him a visit? What a laugh!"

Dan remembered, though with a pang of remorse.

"Yeah," he said. "And you were hobbling around for weeks on that ankle after climbing up, trying to get in to see what he kept in that 'office' of his." His expression relaxed into a grin.

"Crazy idiot!"

"That's me," said Peter, as he jumped up.

"Come on, Sis, we've got to get home. What are you going to do with those chips?"

"I'm going to feed them to the gulls," she said, and threw them up into the air.

There was a tremendous screeching and a flurry of wings, as the gulls dived and swooped to catch each morsel of their windfall in mid-air.

Not a single chip dropped back down to the ground.

CHAPTER SEVEN

The sun beat down on Dan's head as he bent forward to push through the pedals. It was a few days later, and he was cycling up the steep cliff road, on his way to his favourite place to paint.

This is an insane way to spend my time, he thought. *There are probably very few things a person could do voluntarily that cause this much physical pain and suffering. Why am I doing it again?*

But he knew why. Firstly, he knew that somewhere along this journey, there would be a point at which he would come face to face with his true inner character. At the point when he hit "the wall," suddenly, all projections and ideas he had about himself, all the pain about his mother's condition and how their closeness had been stolen since she had become so unwell, all the angst at home with his grandmother, were all stripped away. It was just him, the bike, and the road. At that point, his mind would start to invent all sorts of reasons why it would be okay to stop. It was then he was faced with one of life's greatest questions: would he push through the pain and continue, or succumb and give up?

Ever since the first time Dan had experienced the wall, on this same cliff road, he knew that he needed to practice rising to the challenge. His last successful journey to the top only brought him so far; he had to keep his appointment again with the steep, foreboding route all the way up to the clifftop.

And it was worth it. The reward for finally getting over the rise was truly the most spectacular view for miles around. This was the other reason Dan chose to take this most tortuous of routes. And he still remembered the first ever time he saw the vista open up before him. It had fair taken his breath away.

Beneath a serene, azure sky, the ocean moved, glittering. Billowing white and blue triangles moved in formation-like patterns across the water. Further away, wakes of fast-moving boats criss-crossed like messages written in the waves. To the west, the head curved around the bay like a comforting arm. The quay was an attractive centrepiece, with kiosks and ticket booths for the pleasure boats that were coming and going. Waves foamed as they broke onto a gleaming strip of pale gold. The spots of colour that studded this narrow strip were people, tiny and far away. Parasols fluttered gaily, like frilly buttons.

Dan couldn't hear any sound from the activities down below. There was only the breeze and the occasional call of a seagull, as overhead it wheeled its way around the clifftop and dived back down to the shoreline again.

The prospect spurred Dan on through the time of strain that was now upon him. But there were still nagging thoughts. Couldn't he just take a break? Surely it wouldn't matter this one time. He'd come so far up the road, getting off and pushing wouldn't bring any shame. Just about everyone else who cycled up here would be doing that at this stage.

Heart pumping heavily, perspiring all over, his legs beginning to cramp, he was now cycling into a strong headwind that had just whipped up. Dan felt himself wavering.

Just then, he rounded the bend, and saw the final straight to the rise. He was nearly there. Although each rotation of the pedals felt like agony, he pushed on to the end of the route. He just about kept his balance as he came off the road, passed the barriers and collapsed on the grass verge overlooking the bay.

He lay there panting for quite some time, gazing up at the sky. It was all he could see. There was nothing else, even at the edge of his vision. *Here I can almost touch the sky*, he thought. He felt like he too was floating in that same azure atmosphere. The headwind was now nowhere to be found; it had transformed into a soft, whispering breeze that gently caressed his face. He closed his eyes.

Eventually, his breathing returned to normal. He got up and opened the pack strapped to his bike. After a good drink of water, he pulled out a set of metal rods which assembled into an easel. He then set a small canvas on it. The partially painted scene already clearly mirrored that which was spread out before him. It showed a sensitivity to shape and form, with a keen eye for composition. There was obvious talent here. His teacher had been very complimentary, encouraging him to take his art on to A Level. Dan wasn't that bothered about school, but he'd always wanted to create; to draw and paint. It was in his DNA.

Equipment like paints, brushes, and pallet followed. Once everything was set up, Dan paused to take a few bites of the banana he had brought. Today he wanted to focus on the detail on the beach. The basic shapes in the composition required shading and depth to bring them to life, a brush stroke here, a dab of shadow there. He drew up his camping stool and began.

As he got into more of a rhythm, painting intuitively, his thoughts turned once more to the childhood memory that had been awakened that day at the museum. Dan recalled the warm, playful expression on his father's face, as he had smiled down at him. He experienced again the same sense of love and acceptance. Bitter-sweet though the memory might be in light of events that had followed, the image still made him smile.

He wondered what kind of a person his dad had been. He knew from his mother that he used to tend their flower garden and grow fruits and vegetables. *That garden could certainly do with some of his loving care now,* Dan thought. And he had loved the sea.

Then Dan thought of what he had discovered about the events around the *Tara Belle*. But there were still so many unknowns. Dan couldn't help turning these questions over in his mind.

What had happened to the animal remains? Under what circumstances had his father died? Had he really made a mistake about his analysis? Was he really the discredited marine biologist everyone made him out to be?

Suddenly Dan remembered one of the articles he'd read had mentioned an organization that investigated marine accidents. Maybe it had a report on the *Tara Belle*? He resolved to look into it later.

His musings were brought to an end at the sound of a high-pitched *ping*. Fishing his phone out of his back pocket, he saw that Peter had sent him a message. It read, *Got some news about that dinosaur carcass, etc. I'll tell you about it tomorrow.*

Dan put the phone down. He didn't know what to think. Surely this is what he wanted, to know more. After all, he had just been wondering about the questions he still had. But what if it revealed something negative about his dad? Maybe it was better to just remember him the way his mother had always described him, on the rare occasions she spoke of him: a noble hero lost at sea. What good would it do to dredge up stuff he would prefer to not know, even if it were true? What if the truth would give him even more pain?

But, no, he had to find out, no matter what the consequences. He looked at the painting in front of him and thought about the genetic coding he seemed to have within him to create. Surely, nothing could take that away. Or anything else he had. Surely it was okay to now face this part of his history, another part of his identity.

He said quietly but firmly to himself, "I am Dan Jenkins, the son of William Jenkins, marine biologist, who was lost at sea. Whatever that means."

CHAPTER EIGHT

The next day, before he set off to meet Peter, Dan looked up the accident investigation organization on his computer. On the BMAI website, summaries of current accident investigations were listed:

Grounding and loss of a UK registered fishing vessel… Fall from a gangway on board a UK registered sail training vessel … Collision between UK registered general cargo vessel and German registered bulk carrier… Failure of fishing gear on board a UK registered fishing vessel…

Many of these incidents had fatalities. Dan felt sick as he read through the list. The text above the report request button read as follows:

You can search and request a report for an incident here. Please note, due to the nature of the detail in BMAI reports, you will need to provide proof of age, as recipients need to be over 18 years old.

That was disappointing. As he was only fourteen, Dan knew he wouldn't be able to access the BMAI report any time soon, assuming there was one. In light of that, he was even more keen to hear what Peter had to say.

Peter was waiting for him outside the kiosk by the pontoon.

"Alright?" Dan said.

"Yeah, pretty good. You okay?"

"I'm fine. What's this you were saying about plesiosaur information yesterday?"

It was clear Dan was keen to hear the news. What had Peter found out?

"Well, you know the *Tara Belle* was owned by Chesterton Fisheries?"

"Yeah, like pretty much all the trawlers around here."

"Well, I just happened to mention to Matt that—"

"What do you mean, you happened to mention to Matt? What are you doing talking to Matt about any of this stuff?"

Disappointment crashed in upon Dan.

"I know he's your cousin," he said, "but you must know he's a gormless waste of space. What help could he possibly be?"

This was not the conversation Dan had hoped to be having. Peter looked a bit uncomfortable.

"I know he can be a bit of an idiot sometimes and I didn't mean to tell him anything. It just kind of came out. He didn't say anything much at the time and to be honest I'd forgotten all about it."

Dan glared at him.

"Sorry."

Dan didn't say anything, so Peter continued, "But it may have been a good thing, anyway. You see, Matt had taken note of what I said and, well, you know what Chesterton was like with him when we saw them both last in the café? Well, Matt said he'd like to stick it to Chesterton. Matt reckons he could get his father, who works for Chesterton's as you know, to find out some information about what happened on the *Tara Belle* and pass it on to you."

That floored Dan. It was rather uncharacteristic of Matt to

offer help, but it was probably true his father could have access to such records, should he want to get his hands on them.

"He said to meet him in Jasper's Wood on Friday night, if you want to know more. He reckons he should have found out by then."

Dan was tempted to see what he might come up with. After all, Matt was harmless enough. What did he have to lose?

"Okay," said Dan, "I'll be there."

CHAPTER NINE

Jasper's Wood stood tall and dark in the evening sunshine. It was on a small hill outside Moorton. Leaving their bikes at the bottom, the two boys trudged up the hill path.

Dan thought back to the morning, when he had been researching dinosaurs and plesiosaurs:

Plesiosaurus (Greek: πλησίος (plesios), near to + σαῦρος (sauros), lizard) is a genus of extinct, large marine sauropterygian reptile that lived during the Early Jurassic period. It is known by nearly complete skeletons from the Lias of England. It is distinguishable by its small head, long and slender neck, broad turtle-like body, a short tail, and two pairs of large, elongated paddles...

So began the introductory article he found online. ...

It was so named "near lizard" by William Conybeare and Henry De la Beche, to indicate that it was more like a normal reptile than Ichthyosaurus ("fish lizard"), which had been found in the same rock strata just a few years earlier...Plesiosaurus fed mainly on clams and snails, and is thought to have eaten belemnites, fish and other prey as well. Its U-shaped jaw and sharp teeth would have been like a fish trap. It propelled itself by the paddles, the tail being too short to be of much use. Its neck could have been used as a rudder when navigating during a chase…

Peter and Dan reached the place at the top of the hill where the path entered the wood. Matt was waiting for them, as agreed.

"Alright?" said Dan.

Matt looked past them, to see if anyone was behind.

"This way," he said.

They followed the sealed path for some time. All of a sudden though, Matt veered left and started pushing through the under-growth. They passed through a clearing and then were back to pushing through more foliage. It was mainly soft–bracken and the like–so not too difficult to move through. Another clearing, a right turn and then back for a third time through the trees, which seemed to be getting denser and darker each time.

Dan was concerned. What was going on? How much cloak and dagger was really needed here?

"What's happening? Where are we going?" he asked.

"Not far now,' was Matt's answer, as he pushed on through the vegetation.

Not long after that, Dan perceived a light up ahead. As they drew nearer, he could see that it was yellowy orange. A campfire, maybe? Dan's heart started to pound. Would he really find out what had happened to his father? Dan had hoped for so much, but right now, he felt very unsure.

They entered a large clearing, where a campfire burned in the centre. The boys blinked in the sudden brightness and looked around. A figure stood to one side of the fire. It was Chesterton! *What's going on?* thought Dan. *This isn't what was arranged.*

Chesterton was silent and standing perfectly still, his poker face revealing nothing. All at once, he pulled something out from behind his back. It was a mask. As he put it up to his face, Dan could see it was the head of a reptile.

Suddenly, Chesterton lunged forward, hands claw-like, with a thunderous roar.

"Grrrr! Dinosaur Boy!"

Then out from the shadows appeared many more figures, faces painted or masked, all roaring fiercely.

"Raah! Sea Monster!"

"Dino Boy! Grrrr! Grrrr!"

Dan felt a pang of shame as the group jeered at him, their reptilian faces leering in the firelight. Moving forward, their mockery began to increase in intensity.

"Sea Monster! Grrrr!"

"Raar! Plesiosaur!"

"Sea Serpent! Raar!"

The jeering became louder and louder. Some hands were clawed, others were menacingly clenched into fists, as the grotesque ensemble started to close in around Dan and Peter. Matt had donned a mask and was right in Peter's face.

Dan was alarmed. *What's happening?* he thought in panic. *Are they going to beat us?*

He turned to see Peter recoiling from the advance. But somewhere in the back of Dan's mind, he couldn't help thinking, *This is your fault. I shouldn't have trusted you.*

"What's happening? Why did you bring me here?" he shouted at Peter. "What have you done, you traitor!"

Dan then turned and, with all his strength, forced his way through the rabble to bolt for the shadows. Away from the firelight, he could barely see. Sheer adrenalin drove him forward, he had no idea where, as he pushed through briars and thistles this time. He heard shouts behind but couldn't make out what was said. Panic rose in him—*were they following him?* He tried to run even faster. He stumbled and fell, but scrambled to his feet in an instant, so great was his instinct to escape. Blindly he kept running, punching away branches now, barely registering when they whipped into his face.

From deep inside him anger, pain and frustration welled up into tears that pricked his eyes and blurred his vision. The pain of a beating would have been better than the heartless disregard shown to him by Chesterton's gang. They really were rotten to the core.

The shouts were receding. Dan was relieved, but realized even if he was free from the mob, he had another problem: he had no idea where he was going or how to get out of the wood. And the light was fading. It would be no fun to be lost in Jasper's Wood overnight. Fear rose again, spurring him on. His clothes kept catching on thorns and this time he heard his t-shirt rip as he pulled away. But he had to keep moving. Surely, he would come across a way out at some stage if he just kept going.

He began to tire. The pace was too much to keep up. He realized for the first time how fast he was panting. Pausing to lean against a tree trunk, he gasped for breath. He looked through the trees, as his breathing slowed, trying to make out what was ahead. Was that light he saw? Despite the pain he now felt, he started running again. It must at least be a clearing. The light got brighter and brighter. The trees seemed to fall away with every step he was taking now.

Finally, he burst out beyond the treeline, letting out a howl of pain mixed with anger, shame, and relief. The view of Moorton and the ocean below was no consolation. Cut and bruised, completely exhausted, he collapsed into uncontrollable sobs.

CHAPTER TEN

Kneeling on the garden path, Dan reached for the toolkit and rummaged through it. His bike was propped up against the front garden gate, back wheel off. Carefully he lifted the wheel onto the frame and started to screw it back into position. He was so engrossed in what he was doing, he didn't hear footsteps approaching on the pavement, or see Peter lean over the gate to look at what he was doing.

"Alright, mate?" said Peter.

Dan started at his greeting and looked up. When he saw who it was, his face, still showing the remnants of cuts and bruises, clouded over and he resumed what he was doing.

"What do you want?" he said.

"Well, I thought I'd come to see you—see how you're doing—as you haven't answered any of my messages over the last few days."

"I don't think there's anything to talk about."

Peter looked taken aback.

"What do you mean, nothing to talk about? I haven't seen you since we were in Jasper's Wood. I didn't even know what had happened to you when you left. I had quite a time of it after that, I can tell you."

Dan's anger flared up.

"I don't care what happened to you," he snarled, "It was all a big mistake. How could I have believed you? What was I thinking? You and that wretched cousin of yours making out there was going to be something worthwhile to meet up for—how naïve could I have been to think that?"

Dan was in fact, even more angry with himself and he knew deep down why he had believed Peter. He had so wanted what Peter had said to be true.

He pushed that nagging thought aside and said, "How do you think it feels to have the likes of Chesterton and his mob know about Dad and what the newspapers said about him? Under usual circumstances, I'd never have anything to do with people like them," Dan fumed. "And look what happened! What a bunch of scumbags!"

Dan's eyes pricked with tears. It was as if he were right back there, in the firelight, and he felt the pain as keenly as he had that day in the woods.

"But I didn't know what they had planned," protested Peter. "I thought it was unusual, yes, but I never dreamed they would just want to make a mockery out of it all."

Dan couldn't contain himself.

"I don't believe you!" he spat. "You and Matt knew precisely what was going to happen. You led me like a lamb to the slaughter. You're a traitor! Now, leave me alone!"

Dan got up and opened the gate.

"Get out of my way!" he yelled.

Peter stood aside and Dan pushed past with his bike.

"And don't come back!" said Dan, over his shoulder.

Even as he rode away, Dan knew that Peter hadn't known what Chesterton's gang had lined up for them that day in Jasper's Wood. It didn't make sense, Dan knew, because Peter was a true friend. Dan was being completely unreasonable, and Peter was right to protest at his accusations. But Dan just couldn't bring himself to forgive Peter or himself. The wounds from that day were still too raw.

He was still thinking about these things as he rode past the quay along the beach road. Suddenly there was a shout from the promenade.

"Dan! Wait, Dan!"

Dan slowed and turned to see who it was.

"Dan, wait!"

He stopped. At first, he couldn't see who was calling him, but then he realised an auburn-haired girl was coming towards him. It was Naomi. Dan couldn't believe it. Two Murrays in the same day! The last thing he wanted right now was to have anything to do with Peter's sister.

"What is it?" he said, curtly. "Shouldn't you be with your brother?"

"I know Mum always wants Peter to look after me, but I'm actually perfectly capable of looking after myself. I just wanted to say, I heard about what happened in Jasper's Wood."

Dan cursed under his breath. Did the whole town know what had happened that day?

"Good for you. I hope you had a good laugh," he said, bitterly.

"Well, no, I thought it was awful," said Naomi, surprised. "Peter was very upset, but he says you don't seem to want to talk to him."

"If you're trying to be some sort of go-between, you can forget it."

"Oh, no, I hadn't thought of that," she paused, "although I would be willing—"

Dan glared at her.

"Are we finished?" he said.

Dan's manner had her flustered.

"Er, look, I didn't say anything before, because it looked like

46

you and Peter would find things out your own way. But seeing how things turned out, I wanted to tell you something."

"What do you mean?"

"I think I know how you can find out about your dad."

CHAPTER ELEVEN

With a clear sky, sunlight gleaming on the cars and buses that passed by, and the sea glittering beyond, the view out of the café window looked very different from that gloomy, soggy day, when Dan had first come across the story of the *Tara Belle.*

Naomi was tucking into a banana sundae.

"This is delicious. Thanks so much. Do you want some? I don't think I can eat it all by myself."

"No thanks," Dan replied. "This drink will do just fine. So, tell me, what did you mean about finding out about my dad?"

"Well," said Naomi, trying to wipe the ice-cream from around her mouth, "you know the boat your dad was on was owned by Chesterton Fisheries?"

Dan tried to contain his annoyance.

"Peter and I met with Chesterton's son, if you can call it a meeting, if you recall. Of course I know that."

"Sorry, yes, that's right. Well, you see, my grandfather worked for them for a while, in security."

This began to interest Dan. Maybe Naomi's grandfather would know something.

"It was a while ago. Sometimes Mum and Dad would go with Peter to his sailing events. I hadn't started sailing then."

Dan was confused.

"What's this got to do with Chesterton Fisheries?" he asked.

"Well, Grandad used to take me to his work, you see; when he was looking after me while they were away. I'm not sure he was supposed to, but the other people working there seemed okay with it, if they knew. He was, what's the word he used? Discreet, yes, discreet."

Dan couldn't help smiling to himself, picturing the old man in a uniform trying to hide the little Naomi under a desk or in a cupboard when his colleagues passed by. In reality, it probably wasn't anything like that, of course.

"I'm sure he was very discreet," he said quietly, with the glimmer of a smile.

"Usually, I stayed at the front desk and played on my Nintendo DS, but sometimes I went with him when he went around the building. There wasn't much to do during the day, but I was with him a couple of times in the evening, too. That was when I saw what and how he checked everything."

Dan was rather mystified.

"Why are you telling me this? Does your grandad know something about my dad or not?"

"Well, yes and no."

Dan looked blank.

Naomi seemed to like the fact that she had him at a loss. She grinned, her freckled nose wrinkling.

"No, in that he didn't know your dad, or any of the crew on the *Tara Belle*, in fact. He worked there later." She paused for effect. Dan said nothing. *This is getting painful*, he thought.

"But yes," she went on, "in that he told me he had heard that all the records your dad took of the plesiosaur carcass were stored in the building. They were put in the arc…arc-something."

"Arc? Oh, do you mean archives?" suggested Dan.

"Archives, yes, that's it. They'd all been put in the

archives, along with the other stuff people had written about what happened."

Dan sat back in his seat and whistled under his breath. If what Naomi said was true, this could be a real treasure trove of information to help him find answers. But how could he get to see them?

"Does your grandad still have contact with someone who works there who would help?"

"Oh no. But I visit the offices from time to time after school. They know me there, you see. They always give me a chocolate biscuit and say how big I've grown since the last time I came. You know, the sort of thing aunts say to you."

Dan didn't have an aunt, only an uncle somewhere in America, but he could imagine the sort of thing Naomi was talking about.

"But how does that help?"

"Well," said Naomi, leaning forward and lowering her voice, "I could help you get those records. I know my way around the building. I know where the keys are kept and where the archive room is. I could help you get in and—"

"What, like breaking and entering?" Dan almost shouted in alarm.

"Shhh!" Naomi hissed. "It's probably best not to tell everyone," she whispered.

Dan could hardly believe what he had just heard. This girl must be unhinged. What was she thinking, suggesting that the two of them become criminals?

"Anyway, it wouldn't be *breaking*," she continued. "The whole point, or at least a big part of it, is that I could get into the building sometime earlier and unlock a window or something, so we could get in that way."

Dan's head was in a spin. Naomi wasn't joking about this. She was actually talking about her little plan in all seriousness.

"And we wouldn't necessarily be stealing," she said. "I'm sure we could find a way of returning things anonymously if we wanted to. Besides, whose records are they?"

She had a point. Why did Chesterton Fisheries have possession of his father's work? Dan realised that it could be argued he had the right to it. He pushed that thought to the back of his mind, returning to the absurdity of Naomi's proposal.

"But the security! And what about alarms and CCTV? It would be impossible!" he protested.

"I know all the security, remember? Their routines. Even if they changed them, I don't think they would vary that much. And they've never had any alarms. Old Chesterton isn't known for spending money if he doesn't think it's necessary. 'No expense spent!' Grandad used to joke about it. If anything has changed, and worst case, an alarm goes off, I'll be stuck inside making up an excuse for being there, while you scarper."

Naomi looked at Dan. He didn't look at all convinced.

"Don't you want to find out about your dad?" she appealed. "Come on, it'd be fun!"

Fun was the last thing Dan thought it would be. He was reminded of how uneasy he'd felt just accompanying Peter when he tried to get into Whiskey Wainwright's place. And to this day he felt sick at the thought that they might have been seen as they ran away. How could he possibly go on a lark like this?

"Maybe we're looking at this all wrong. Maybe we should just ask to see the records," he said.

But even as the words came out of his mouth, he knew there was no way he wanted to have anything more to do with the Chestertons. He couldn't imagine Mr. Chesterton being some kind of benevolent benefactor, in stark contrast to his son. Naomi confirmed his suspicions.

"Oh no, you wouldn't be able to do that. No one in the business will help. Those things are under lock and key for a reason."

"What reason?"

"I don't know. But we can find out, can't we?"

Could they find out? Was it really possible? The whole idea of breaking into the Chesterton Fisheries building was utter anathema to Dan. But on the other hand, if Naomi really knew her way around the place like she said she did, the possibility of getting his father's work seemed almost within his reach, tempting him like a shining treasure just beyond the grasp of an intrepid explorer.

In turmoil, Dan put his head in his hands.

It was all wrong. And there was certainly a chance that they would be discovered. But surely, he had to try. And wouldn't he always regret it if he didn't?

After a few more moments of deliberation, he looked up, resolute.

"Okay," he said, "let's do it."

CHAPTER TWELVE

It was the night Naomi and Dan had agreed to go to Chesterton Fisheries. At dusk Dan arrived at the corner of the road where the business had its main offices. Getting away from home had been straight forward. His grandmother had been in the living room, in front of the TV with her tea and crossword, as usual. Dan had been able to slip out unnoticed.

Naomi was already there. She stepped out of the shadows as he cycled up.

"This would be a good place to stow the bike," she said in a loud whisper, gesturing to the bushes behind her. Dan wasn't quite sure it was necessary to hide his bike but he pushed it into the bushes anyway. He figured it probably wouldn't hurt, and he knew he was very much under Naomi's direction on this "mission", as she called it.

"It's like *Mission Impossible*," she had beamed, when they had been making their plans.

Mission? Kind of. Impossible? It certainly felt surreal as they made their way along the street to the beginning of the wire fencing that surrounded the Chesterton Fisheries site. Further along, there was a driveway blocked by a padlocked gate. They walked past the driveway, pausing in the shadow of a tree, away from the streetlights. They were standing in front of a pedestrian gate.

Beyond, they could see the glassed reception area. No one could be seen there. Naomi looked up and down the street. Everything was quiet.

"The vehicular gate is locked at night, but they only keep the pedestrian gate shut, not locked," Naomi had told Dan beforehand. Sure enough, when she tried the handle, the gate quietly swung open.

Naomi led the way down the side of the building, careful to keep in the shadow of the fence. *I'm really here*, Dan thought. *I'm really trespassing on private property.* He reflected that although that was true, it felt very normal walking around the building. Apart from the keeping in the shadows bit. They reached the far corner of the building where there were some bushes and Naomi pulled him down into them.

"This bit is a blind spot for the cameras," she whispered. "I remember how Granddad and the others used to complain about it. We're going to get in through that window up there," she pointed.

Dan could just make out a set of two frosted windows. The lower one was large and squarish, the one above it was the same width, but only about a foot high.

"Which window?"

"The top one. The fanlight."

"But how?"

"It's the ladies' loos. I paid a visit to the office today and went in there. The catch on the top window should be off. The lower one doesn't open."

"I couldn't fit through that even if I could get up there," protested Dan.

"Not a problem. I can get through. Then I'll let you in the side door back there."

Dan didn't know whether to disbelieve her or admire her. Admiration won out.

Give us a leg up.

She tried to reach the window with her foot supported by his cupped hands, but in the end, she had to balance on his shoulders. Dan looked up. Naomi had prised the window open. It didn't look like it opened very wide. Naomi pushed her head through, then wriggled her shoulders past the frame. As she twisted to get her arms through as well, she whispered, "Give us a push!"

This is where it all goes horribly wrong, thought Dan, as he pushed. *There's going to be an almighty crash.* He looked up to see Naomi inside as far as her waist. Through the frosted glass he saw her then bend double, head down, arms outstretched to support herself as she gently slid down into what were, he found out later, a bunch of washbasins.

He pulled back into the shadows and waited. It seemed like an age before he heard a soft click and saw a door open. He made his way to it as quickly and quietly as he could. He was nearly there when it occurred to him, *What if it's not Naomi? It could be someone else.* He stopped, heart racing, and listened. After some time, a head popped around the edge of the door.

"Dan, are you there?"

Relieved, Dan moved forward.

"Here I am," he whispered, and stepped inside.

CHAPTER THIRTEEN

The corridor was dark, except for some emergency lighting.

"Did you bring a torch?" whispered Naomi.

"Here," replied Dan, pulling one out of his pocket. "You?"

"On my phone. Keep it handy. I'll check around the corner."

Naomi edged along the right-hand wall and poked her head into the hallway. Returning she said," I can see the reception lights on at the end of the corridor. I didn't see anyone, but I presume they're sitting at the desk at the moment. The keys are in the office just behind reception. I'll go and get them now."

She spoke so matter-of-factly about the situation. Standing inside the building now, Dan was struck anew that what they were doing was extremely risky.

"What if someone comes down the hallway? Won't they see you?"

He could just make out her countenance. She was grinning!

"I'll be alright. Don't worry."

It really was a game to her, Dan marvelled, as he watched her disappear around the corner.

More waiting. He couldn't hear anything. He figured that was a good sign. He was tempted to look down the hallway to see what was going on. Edging to the corner, he took a peek. The light from the reception area seemed to light up the hallway considerably. It didn't occur to Dan that things would look much darker to someone coming the other way, with the light behind them. He was just in time to see Naomi come out of a room at the end of the hallway, quietly shutting the door behind her. She then edged along the wall towards him, pausing in each doorway. Suddenly someone coughed with a low gravelly voice. Dan's heart missed a beat. Naomi moved quickly down the rest of the hallway and around the corner. They both stood perfectly still, listening. Nothing. Dan let out a sigh of relief and looked at Naomi. She grinned silently, holding up a fob, with a key dangling from it.

"This way," she whispered.

She was about to step back into the hallway when there was more noise from the reception area. A chair moving, maybe? And then footsteps–first shuffling and then the sound of someone walking around on the hard floor. Then the steps became regular, albeit more muffled on the hallway carpet tiles. They were getting nearer. They paused from time to time, and then there was a rattling sound. Locked doors were being tested, Dan thought, as he looked around in panic, his heart starting to thump. How would they avoid discovery?

He felt his arm being grabbed. As he stepped back to regain his balance, he was shoved further back against something hard. It poked uncomfortably into his back. Then even the emergency lighting disappeared and they were in total darkness. Naomi had shut them inside a cupboard. He heard the sound of a key turning in the lock. The footsteps were very close now. Dan pictured the security guard walking around the corner into the corridor. Next thing he knew, the handle of the cupboard door was rattling. Dan froze in terror, his heart now beating so fast he thought it would burst. After what seemed like an eternity, the rattling stopped and the footsteps started up again, receding this time. Dan felt weak. He now registered the pain in his back, which was considerable. He tried to move out of the way of the object digging into him, but there seemed to be obstacles blocking him on every side.

"I think it's best we stay here until he's done his rounds," came Naomi's whisper in the darkness. "We should have a good chunk of time to get around once he's finished."

Dan didn't like what he heard, but knew it was probably sensible.

"Okay."

They waited as still and quietly as they could. Finally, they heard footsteps coming back up the hallway. They passed by, continuing towards the reception area. Then there was shuffling and the movement of a chair again. Another cough. Then silence.

The two of them waited another minute or so and then Naomi unlocked the cupboard door. They slipped out, making for the hallway, turning left this time.

Dan couldn't help thinking that Naomi was using what would become "vocational talents." Either she would end up being some kind of high-end cat burglar, or maybe she'd end up working in government espionage, on the right side of the law instead. Sort of.

At the end of the hall was a door.

"This is it," Naomi said, as they reached it.

She tried to put the key in the lock. It didn't fit. She tried it again, several times. Dan was concerned she was making too much noise.

"Are you sure you've got the right key?" he whispered, a bit too loudly.

"Yes, absolutely sure. The fob says it's for the archive room."

She tried the key a couple more times and then stopped.

"Why isn't it working?" she whispered to herself.

She thought for a moment or two, and then got out her phone. Dan wondered what she was doing. This was no time to make a call. Then she switched on the torch and shone it at the sign on the door.

Computer Room, it read.

Naomi gasped. Dan thought he might need to revise his opinion of Naomi's vocational skills.

"I remember, now," she whispered. "The archive room *is* at the end of the hallway. But it's on the first floor, not the ground floor."

Dan was relieved. They were still in business. Naomi led the way back up the hallway to where there were glass double doors to the stairwell. As he followed, Dan tripped on something in the dark. Reaching his hand out to the wall for balance, he dropped his torch. It fell with a dull thud. Unfortunately though, it didn't stop there, but started to roll down the hallway towards the reception area. Dan watched in disbelief, unable to move. The torch came to rest beyond the shadows, in full view of anyone who happened to look down the hallway.

Naomi started to head towards it, but Dan stopped her. He knew this challenge was for him. He couldn't leave it up to Naomi to get him out of trouble this time, although no doubt she'd find it easier and probably do a better job. It was up to him to retrieve the torch.

"I'll go," he whispered.

Dan started to edge along the hallway. He could hear movement in the reception area. It was probably just the security guard moving in his chair, but it was enough to unnerve him and make him pause. His mouth was dry. He tried to swallow, but to no avail. Steeling his resolve, he began moving forward again. Slowly, carefully, he edged his way towards the torch. *Just focus on the torch,* he told himself. That made things easier. A few more steps and he had reached as far as he could go in the shadows.

He paused to listen. All was quiet. That meant he had to retrieve his torch in absolute silence. *You can do this, Dan Jenkins,* he told himself. At that moment, he suddenly felt completely calm. In one movement, he stepped noiselessly into the torch and stooped down to pick up the torch. Then, without a moment's hesitation, he turned and walked briskly back to the stairwell doors.

The right door made quite a creak. Moving it slowly only seemed to make it worse. The left door was the same. So, Naomi gave up and pushed through as quickly as she could. Every step seemed to echo around the stairwell. Dan hoped the sound wasn't reaching the ears of the security guard. The two of them tiptoed up one flight of stairs and then another, to open the door onto the first floor.

They headed to the far end of the hallway. Another door. Naomi tried the key. Dan held his breath. It worked. The lock clicked and the door swung open. They stepped in, quietly closing the door behind them.

They didn't risk turning the overhead light on. The room was stacked, floor to ceiling, with cardboard archive boxes. They varied in size, but similar sizes were stacked on top of each other, and they all appeared to be clearly labelled.

"You start that end and I'll start this end," whispered Naomi.

Dan shone his torch down the first stack of boxes. They all seemed to be financial and tax records. The second stack was the same. Then there were some equipment files, records to do with safety and boats' logs, insurance etc. All rather unpromising. But then, Dan reminded himself, *This place could have the secrets of my father's last hours.* For a moment he imagined himself in a magical cave that held hidden treasures for him to discover. He refocussed, carefully checking every single label, in the hope that it might be the one that would bring him success.

They worked in silence for a while. Then Dan heard a gasp from the other side of the room.

"Dan, I think I've found it!"

Dan came over and looked at the box with Naomi. He could hardly believe it. There in black and white was exactly what he had been looking for. The label said *Tara Belle records August 1999.*

"That was the month my father died," whispered Dan.

The archive box was near the bottom of the stack, so they removed the boxes on top as quickly and quietly as they could.

Dan paused. What was he about to find out?

"Open it!" urged Naomi.

Dan grabbed the lid. It was jammed on tightly, so he had to maneuver it off with quite a bit of effort.

Finally, it came loose, and he laid it down, shining his torch inside the box.

It was empty.

CHAPTER FOURTEEN

The two-year-old Dan hid shyly behind his mother as she opened the door. Two rough-looking fishermen stood there. He could see the concerned looks on their faces. They spoke in hushed tones...

Dan woke with a start. Momentarily disorientated, he looked around his dark room. He realized he'd been dreaming. He now remembered the fishermen's visit. As he thought it over, he understood, with greater depth now, the bowed heads and the sympathetic gestures. His father, from that day on, would never come home again.

He turned over, trying to get back to sleep. But as he lay there, thoughts of the night before came flooding back. After their discovery of the box in the archive room, leaving the premises was all a bit of a blur. In a kind of dream-like sequence, the two of them had appeared to effortlessly make their way down the stairs and back along the hall.

There had been no problem going out through the side door and, keeping in the shadow of the fence, away from the street lighting, they had moved noiselessly towards the front of the building. They had waited until the security guard had left the reception area again, before leaving through the pedestrian gate. At the corner of the street, they silently went their separate ways. There didn't seem anything to say. Dan realized now that he hadn't even thanked Naomi for her help.

It all seemed so unbelievable. Had it really happened, he wondered? Lying there in his bedroom, surrounded by all that was ordinary and familiar, it was hard to believe that he and Naomi had done something so outrageous just a few hours earlier. But it was true. And the disappointment of the outcome was hard to bear.

Dan thought back over the last days and weeks: the museum guide's tale and the re-surfacing of his earliest memory—that encounter with his father, his visit and appeal to his mother, his research, the debacle in Jasper's Wood and finally this night-time visit to Chesterton Fisheries. All for nothing. He wondered what he could possibly do now. As far as he knew, he had exhausted all avenues of enquiry. "Exhausted" was a good word, he thought. That's how he felt. And he really was at the end of the line.

Game over, he thought, succumbing to the cloud of depression as it enveloped him.

He dozed.

Birdsong woke him. The delicate, melodious chirruping was really quite beautiful, soothing his soul. Daylight moved on the floor from behind the drawn curtains. He rolled over to check the time. It was 7:30 a.m. With an immense effort, he roused himself, trying to shake off his gloominess.

I know, he thought, *I'll go up to East Cliff and paint. I always feel better there.* He got up and started to get ready.

It was another idyllic day. With a heavy heart, Dan had pedalled the familiar route through Moorton and had started up the cliff road. But he found he didn't have the usual energy to cycle to the top. He had to get off his bike and push it for at least half the way. That was quite demoralizing.

When he finally reached the top and set up to paint, he couldn't focus on the image, even though it was nearly done. It only needed a few highlights and finishing touches, but whatever he tried to do didn't seem to work. His thoughts returned to the disappointment of the night before. The sight of that empty archive box was seared into his memory. What an apt symbol of his experience!

He looked at the canvas on the easel. He thought how the sunny, carefree image was deceptive; it bore no relation to his life, his world. Anger and loathing bubbled up from somewhere deep inside. What was the point of this stupid painting? Nothing he tried ever worked. He probably *was* the son of a failed marine biologist who couldn't tell the difference between a plesiosaur and a basking shark. And he was stuck here in Moorton, with an ailing mother and a dragon of a grandmother. Life couldn't look bleaker.

"What's the point of *you*?" he shouted at the painting.

He squeezed a dark colour onto his palette and started stabbing it onto the painting with his brush.

"You lie! You're not real. You're not going to make any difference. Just like everything else!"

He kept on until he'd all but completely obliterated the picture with dark splotches. Then he grabbed the canvas and with a mighty lunge threw it off the cliff. The sound echoed as it clattered all the way down to the beach below.

CHAPTER FIFTEEN

When Dan got home, he realized he'd had no plan other than to get through the front door. Now that he was here, he actually didn't know what to do. He didn't want to go upstairs to his room. He didn't want to go to the kitchen, or anywhere else in the house, for that matter. He could go neither forward nor backwards. He was empty, at a standstill. So, he stood in the hallway, motionless. That seemed like the only logical thing to do.

All was quiet. *No one home*, he thought. *Good*. He really couldn't face talking to anyone right now. He stood there for a while longer and then he remembered something. In the living room, which had become his grandmother's domain, among the handful of photos on the mantelpiece, was a wedding photo of his parents. It was one of the very few pictures of his father on display. All of a sudden, he really wanted to look at that image again. After all he'd been through over the last few weeks, it was still the closest link he had.

He went into the living room. There it was on the mantelpiece, as always: a framed photo of a smiling couple standing in the entrance to a church. His mother looked so young, cheeks flushed and eyes shining as she clasped her modest bouquet in one hand, resting the other on her husband's arm. Dan mused how he'd probably look just as awkward in a suit as his father did. Yet there was no denying, the young man in the photo looked very happy, for all that.

He recalled one more time the childhood memory of his father's face smiling down at him, his eyes full of playfulness and affection. A wave of despair came over him.

Just then, a noise startled him. He dropped the photo. The glass shattered. He looked up to see his grandmother in the doorway, carrying a tea tray.

"What have you done?" she scolded. "What are you doing, making a mess in here?

She put down the tray, clearly annoyed.

"I didn't know you had come home," she said. "You must have been very quiet coming in." Her tone appeared accusatory.

Dan's anger flared up. He couldn't help but blurt out, "That's rich coming from you. I thought you were out when I didn't hear anything. You're the one sneaking around."

Gran looked taken aback. This was aggressive, even by Dan's usual standards.

"I'd appreciate it if you'd speak to me with some respect, young man. I was sorting out your mother's medication, if you must know. It looks like she'll be coming back home in the next day or so. And preparing medication is a very responsible job that requires a lot of concentration."

Despite the good news of his mother's return, Dan couldn't help sneering, "Yes, too responsible for anyone else to do. Why don't you let me do it? And stop calling me 'young man'. It's clear you don't think I am one, the way you always treat me like a kid. I'm nearly fifteen. When we were on our own, I used to help Mum—even more so when she started to get sick. We'd have been just fine without you!"

"But you were just a kid! You didn't understand the seriousness of her condition. You weren't mindful of your mother's health or safety. I remember, there was that time when you left your stuff on the stairs. Your mum nearly broke her neck falling over it. I knew then you couldn't be trusted around her. It was up to me to look after her. I had to protect her."

Guilt flooded Dan as he remembered the incident, but then he thought, *That was a one-off. I learnt my lesson.*

"But that was ages ago, not long after you moved in," he said. "Have I ever done anything like that since?"

"Well, no, I suppose not. But I couldn't risk it. I couldn't let anything hazardous near her. I had to protect her."

"Even from her own son!"

"Yes, even from her own son," she admitted. "Your father was just the same," she continued, gesturing to the photo on the floor.

"What do you mean?" said Dan, angrily.

"I know it's not good to speak ill of the dead, but the truth is that he was extremely irresponsible, jaunting around the place like some sort of explorer, when he had a wife and family at home. He should have settled down after they were at university and just stuck with the job he had. It was a very good job, too. But no, instead of being sensible, he had to be finding out more about the world, egged on by the likes of that John Wainwright."

Dan was shocked. *Not Whiskey Wainwright*, he thought, *surely not*. If that man had any connection with his father, that was definitely mixed news.

"Do you mean the Wainwright who has his hut down on the beach?" asked Dan, hoping the answer would be in the negative.

"Yes, that's him. I haven't seen him for a long time, mind. I used to know him years ago, when I was growing up here in Moorton. But he was the sort that egged your father on with his research."

She paused, anger clearly starting to show on her face.

"He should never have gone out on that wretched boat," she

exploded. "Whatever kind of accident he had; it would never have happened if he'd stayed here in Moorton. Your mother was never the same again. And losing the baby, too."

Her hands reached out and fluttered over the tea tray for a moment. Then she noticed the look on his face.

"What, you didn't know? Yes, your mum had a miscarriage as well. I'm sure it was the shock of it all. You would have had a little sister," she said, without sympathy.

His legs felt weak. He sank into the nearest chair. He'd had a sister. *Why did Mum never tell me about that? Is there anything else she didn't tell me?* he thought.

"The miscarriage is just another thing that went wrong after that. She was fine before, but your mum's health was never right from then on. I'm sure that's why she's so ill now. Your father's irresponsibility cost the family everything: a husband, a father, a daughter and your mum's health. Destroying all our lives."

Dan was astonished. Did his grandmother really believe his father was to blame for all that?

"But it was an accident! He didn't mean for any of that to happen," he protested.

"It was unforgivable, his going off like that," Gran insisted. "And if it wasn't for your mother, I'd tear that picture of him into pieces and throw it in the bin!"

Dan gasped.

"Don't look at me like that!" she said.

"Anyway, I've had just about enough of you, young man. You can get out of my sight!"

CHAPTER SIXTEEN

Dan took a sip of his coke. Leaving the house after his argument with Gran, he'd ended up back at his usual haunt, the promenade café.

He was shocked at what his grandmother had revealed that day. How she must truly resent her son-in-law, laying all that misfortune at his door. Dan shook his head. Stupid woman. How could she think like that?

But then he remembered something. During that angry exchange, Gran had disclosed something that could potentially help Dan find out about his father: his relationship with John Wainwright.

Thinking of the Wainwright he knew about, with his ramshackle "business" down by the beach, Dan found it hard to believe that anything useful could come from that boozy old man. Was it really worth the risk to approach him about his father and the *Tara Belle*?

What if he recognised Dan from the time he had been there with Peter? Dan didn't know that things wouldn't turn nasty. What if, even if Wainwright did know something, he was the sort of person who would refuse to divulge anything, out of spite? And it was possible he didn't know anything, anyway. It could be a very costly visit, whichever way you looked at it.

On the other hand, what if he did know something, and was

willing to tell? Could Dan live with himself not approaching Wainwright, knowing that this person might have information that could help him put the pieces of this puzzle together?

In the end, Dan knew he would have to go, whatever the outcome. He couldn't leave any stone unturned.

Tomorrow, he decided, *I'll go tomorrow.*

He got up from his seat to leave. Just at that moment, the door opened, and Chesterton and his gang came in.

Dan's first reaction was to try to hide. But there was nowhere to go. He steeled himself, eyes forward, and walked up to the counter.

"Can I pay the bill, please," he said.

Chesterton must have seen him but, to Dan's relief, he'd obviously decided to not acknowledge him. He had other fish to fry.

Dan knew the boys would be planning some sort of pilfering, just like the last time he'd seen them there. He was incensed that they kept getting away with it. And he suddenly had an idea.

"Actually, could I have one of those cookies, too?" he asked.

He moved along the counter and sat on a stool right in front of the cookie jar, while the woman put one on a plate. The other boys, unprepared for this maneuvre, had to move out of his way. Dan sat in front of the jar and started to eat. Even this fairly mild opposition he was offering caused him to quake inside. He did all he could to make sure it didn't show though.

The other boys were silent. Dan had noticed Matt among them. Despite his natural inclination to the contrary, it occurred to him that this was the time he needed to confront Peter's cousin somehow. He had no idea what he would say as, summoning all his courage, he turned around to face him.

"Hello, Matt," he heard himself say. "Haven't seen you since our party the other Friday night. That was pretty good craic. Thanks so much for the invitation."

Matt looked down sheepishly and said nothing.

"And you've brought all your friends here today, too," said Dan. His gaze turned to the boy standing next to Matt. No masks this time. *I'm not afraid of you,* he thought. He ensured he made eye-contact before he moved on, gathering in confidence as he looked at each boy in turn.

Finally, he came to Chesterton himself, who sneered, "Well, if it isn't Jenkins the giant lizard lover. Found any sea monsters recently, Dinosaur Boy?" When he got no response he added, "Daddy would be proud."

Dan saw red. In a flash, he found himself off his seat, within inches of the bully's face.

"Is that the best you can do?" Dan snapped. He didn't wait for an answer. "At least I don't need to throw my weight around and keep a bunch of fawning retards in tow to make me feel like I'm anything better than a nauseating piece of garbage!"

Chesterton glared at him, clearly taken aback. Dan turned and resumed his seat, inwardly shaking with anger.

He continued eating, crumb by slow crumb. Some of the boys shifted their weight awkwardly from one foot to another, unsure of what to do. Their plan was being thwarted and waiting around was becoming embarrassing.

It was time for Chesterton to make a move.

"White tea to takeaway," he said to the woman behind the counter. "Two sugars."

A minute later, the whole crowd of them was gone. Dan breathed a sigh of relief. He knew he had won a victory. What he didn't know then, however, was that Chesterton and his gang would steer clear of him from that day forward.

In a more mellow mood, cycling home through the streets of Moorton, Dan thought of the latest news about his mother.

Even though resuming her care would mean more work, and probably more strain in the household, Dan still revelled in the knowledge that his mum would be back home very soon to start her rehabilitation.

Could his mother indeed get better? Hope dawned in Dan's soul like the first warmth of the sun in springtime. He had hardly dared believe it was a possibility. But even if there were only the slenderest of chances, he resolved that, as far as it was up to him, he would do everything in his power to make it become a reality.

In the meantime, he had the prospect of meeting Whiskey Wainwright in the morning.

CHAPTER SEVENTEEN

To describe John Wainwright's business as the "hut down on the beach" was a little unfair. At the west end of the promenade, tucked under the shadow of the cliff, was an area bordered by a wooden fence. The sign on the fence said *Wainwright Marine.* Beyond the fence was a working yard with a slipway into the sea. There were various items of equipment there and several boats in the process of repair. On the far side of the yard there was a rather ramshackle wooden cabin.

Dan contemplated the scene. Never in a million years would he have imagined coming back here, let alone under these circumstances. *Is this really such a good idea?* he wondered.

He skirted around the side, where the fence ran behind the cabin. Stepping up onto a fence support, he craned his neck to see if anyone was in there. From that angle it was hard to tell. He stepped down again and looked around.

What are you going to do, Dan Jenkins? he asked himself. *You came here to get answers. You're not going to find any standing out here, that's for sure. Now, stop procrastinating and get on with it!*

Dan walked up to the gate and pushed it open. He quietly made his way, past the line of boats, towards the cabin. As he approached, he heard a noise to his left. Before he had a chance to turn, a weathered, burly, bearded man emerged from behind one of the boats. The two of them started. There was a moment's silence and then the man said, "What do you want?"

Images of when he'd last been in the boat yard flooded Dan's mind. Panic suddenly gripped him. His mind went blank and he completely forgot why he was there.

"Well, what is it? I haven't got all day, you know," John Wainwright snapped. He stood tall, foreboding, arms folded across his chest.

When Dan still gave him no response he said, "Right, that's it. If you've got no business here, you need to get out."

He started moving towards Dan, who instinctively backed towards the gate. *I need to say something. I need to say something,* thought Dan, in a panic. But he couldn't think straight.

Suddenly the man stopped.

"Say, haven't I seen you here before?" he said. Dan could see him trying to remember.

That was it. That was enough to shock Dan into a response.

"N-no, I've never been here before," he lied.

The man didn't look convinced and started towards him again. Then Dan could see, from the look on his face, he'd remembered.

"I remember now. You're one of the scumbag vandals who tried to break into my cabin!"

The man lunged at him, grabbed him by the collar and lifted him right off the ground and back against the fence.

"N-no, that wasn't me," panicked Dan.

He knew this was his last chance.

In desperation, he blurted out, "Eleanor Brightman sent me!"

Inside the cabin, the man turned to Dan and asked, suspiciously, "How do you know Eleanor?"

"She's my grandmother," Dan said.

Thinking he probably should provide as much information as he could, he continued, "She used to live in Lymchester, but she's widowed now and lives with me and my mum here in Moorton."

He hesitated.

"She said you knew my father–Will Jenkins."

John's expression changed, softening.

"You'd better sit down," he said.

Dan looked around. He could see only one chair drawn up to the small laminated table. Not wanting to cause any ripples in this newfound calm between them though, Dan sat down on it without a word.

John was lighting a gas ring under a kettle. Then he pulled a stool out from under the table. As he sat down, he drew a tin of tobacco from his pocket.

"I knew your grandmother years ago," he began. "Did she tell you we were sweethearts?"

Dan gasped. He hadn't expected that.

"No, no, she never said that."

"Well, I suppose that's understandable. I thought the world of her, you see, but I let her down. I was a bit wild in my younger days. Got into quite a bit of trouble. The drink didn't help. She deserved better than that."

He started to put tobacco in his cigarette paper.

"She was right to marry Ken Brightman. He was a solid, sensible chap. I'm sure he never got into any trouble. And I'm sure she's better off now, even as a widow, than she ever would have been with me in all my glory."

John spread his arms wide, gesturing to the contents of the cabin. It was just as ramshackle inside as it looked from the outside, Dan thought. Unpainted and very basically furnished, the walls were filled top to bottom with shelves full of tools, small parts, tins of paint, oil, varnish, boat manuals, parts catalogues, and the like. And there was, what looked like, a trestle bed at the far end.

Not pretty, thought Dan, *but probably very practical*. And he realized, the nickname *Whiskey Wainwright* might be a misnomer. If the demon drink had any influence on this man's life these days, it wasn't at all obvious.

"Anyway," resumed John, "it's true, I did know Will. It was when I was working for Chesterton's. That was all a while back. Quite a few years, in fact. Will was a good man. What did you want to know?"

It felt odd to Dan, hearing a man speak about his dad. He realized, all his life what little he'd heard had only ever been from women's perspectives. It felt very different, sitting there listening to John. And now, after all the events of the last few weeks, he finally had someone asking him what he wanted to know. Was he really standing at an open door?

He took a deep breath and said, "I want to know what happened the day he died."

John said nothing at first, but the expression on his face was one of sadness.

"Alright," he said, quietly. The kettle started to whistle, so he got up to turn the gas off and make the tea. Once he'd finished, he brought two mugs to the table.

"No sugar, I'm afraid," he said.

"That's fine. Thanks," said Dan, as he took the mug offered to him.

Seated again, John lit the rolled cigarette and took a sip from his mug. Then he began.

"It must be at least a decade ago—"

"Twelve years," interrupted Dan.

"Twelve years. Yes, that would be about right. It was in the summer—August. I was working on the *Tara Belle*, as I often did at that time. It was a good crew, working under a pretty good captain–Brownrigg was his name, Joseph Brownrigg.

"Will had just come along for the ride, that day. He didn't work for Chesterton's, you see. He was a marine biologist, working on his PhD at the time. He was travelling with us to check out an area where he thought he might be able to get samples for his thesis. He'd been out with us a few times before when we'd been trawling in different areas.

"Anyway, we were about 30 miles offshore when we brought up this very strange creature in our nets. It was dead. Will said later he thought it had been dead for about a month, and although it had started to decay, most of it was still intact. No one in the crew could say for sure what they thought it was, because none of us had seen anything like it before. It was about three metres long, or so. On closer inspection, because it had the four flippers, Will thought it might be some kind of plesiosaur-like mammal. Probably a young one, in light of its size. Credit to the captain, he supported Will's suggestion to take it below deck for analysis.

Being a fishing vessel, we obviously weren't set up for research of that sort, so Will had to improvise. He had to do things old school. The largest area below deck was the galley. It had a dining table that could seat most members of the crew at one time, so that was where Will set up and we moved the carcass down there. The cook was none too pleased, I can tell you," John chuckled. "It didn't smell too good, either."

"Anyway, he was down there for the rest of the day, inspecting the specimen and writing a report. We'd just brought in a good catch, and all was going well, when the winch started to have problems. A pulley broke free from its fixings. We were struggling to make it fast again, so the alarm was sounded to get everyone on deck to help."

John sighed.

"It was such bad timing, and everything happened so quickly. We'd actually got the pulley back into position, and I thought it had been made fast. But just as Will appeared on deck, pulling his lifejacket on, the pulley broke free again. It rocketed across the deck and hit Will on the side of the head. It hit him with such force that he was knocked overboard."

John looked intently down into his mug.

"Terrible," he said, in a husky voice.

The two of them sat in silence for a moment. Dan felt like someone had hit him with great force too. Right in the pit of his stomach.

After letting out a long, deep sigh, John continued.

"From the deck we could see Will in the water. He was unresponsive to our calls and attempts to throw him a line."

"He hadn't managed to finish putting on his life jacket before he was hit, and it had floated free in the water before too long. While we were lowering the life raft, he disappeared. Despite our best efforts to find him, long after the light had gone, it was to no avail. I don't think his body was ever found."

Dan felt sick. A wave of sadness washed over him. He sighed and closed his eyes. He had known how the story ended but hearing the stark details for the first time seemed to make it worse.

"I'm sorry," came John's voice, from a distance, it seemed. "If it's any consolation, I'm sure your father didn't suffer."

Dan roused himself.

"No, thank you for telling me. It's been so hard to find out what happened that day on the *Tara Belle*."

After a long time, he finally took a sip of his tea.

"It's the same for the carcass. I mean, what happened to all Dad's work? I know people would be interested because it could be about a plesiosaur find, but it was also the last thing my father did before he died. Official reports say he made a mistake, but I'd sure like to see his work for myself."

"Isn't it held by Chesterton Fisheries?" John asked.

"It's supposed to be—" Dan realised he might need to be careful what he said here.

"But it's not," he said flatly.

"Well, after the accident, I gathered all Will's notes together from the galley," said John. "He'd taken photos on his camera, too. I figured they should be put in the hands of someone who could let the world know about what he had discovered. So, once we got back to port, I took them to the local newspaper. They were very interested. And I'm glad I did that, because the carcass mysteriously disappeared not long after that."

"What do you think happened there? I mean, how could something like that just go missing?" asked Dan.

"I don't know for sure, but I would guess it was Vested Interests. You see, the plesiosaur discovery only served to put the spotlight on the *Tara Belle* at a time when questions were being asked about the business' equipment maintenance and safety, as well as its operational procedures. Chesterton's has never had the best safety record. And your father's death, well, it showed things weren't right. It was hushed up. Details kept out of the papers and such. As for the carcass, my money's on Mr Chesterton persuading Captain Brownrigg to dispose of it in the hope that everything would blow over as far as public attention was concerned.

"And their plan would probably have worked, if I hadn't taken the papers out of the galley and given them, with the camera, to my journalist friend when we got back to port. But instead, the story made international news. It would have gone further than that, I reckon, if it hadn't been for the 'experts' who came down from London. That's when Mr. Chesterton said the notes were Chesterton Fisheries' property and that the newspaper had to return them. Well, the London experts–*Men in Black*, I call them—looked at your dad's work just long enough to announce it was all a misidentification. However, I'm sure their jobs–and the careers of a whole lot of other scientists and academics–wouldn't have looked so secure if it could have been shown that there are plesiosaurs still swimming around in the seas today. It would have suited them very well to join forces with Mr Chesterton and come down to put the tin hat on your dad's analysis."

Dan's focus became keener.

"So, you don't think Dad made a mistake with his identification? You don't think it was a hoax, like the papers said afterwards?"

"Well, all the members of the *Tara Belle* crew saw the carcass with their own eyes. None of us could reconcile the official report with what we had seen. And I can understand that you of all people would want to see Will's work on the carcass. Then you could weigh up the evidence for yourself."

"I'd love to do that!" protested Dan. "But the papers aren't at Chesterton Fisheries."

"No, they wouldn't be," said John, getting up and opening a drawer in a long chest behind him.

"After they went into archive at Chesterton's, I wasn't convinced that the Vested Interests wouldn't want to have them 'disappeared,' just like the carcass itself. So, I took what you might call, precautionary measures."

He lifted something out of the drawer and put it on the table in front of Dan.

"I decided it would be better if I took them for safekeeping."

CHAPTER EIGHTEEN

Dan looked at the portfolio cover on the table before him. He could hardly believe his eyes. All his searching and questioning, all his pain and risk-taking, had left him empty-handed. He had all but given up on finding his father's work. Yet now apparently here it was right in front of him.

He heard John say, "I've tried to keep them in good condition, so I thought something to keep the dust off would be a good idea. Take your time, there's no rush. I'll be outside, when you're ready."

Dan looked up to see him open the cabin door.

"Basking shark, my arse," said John under his breath, as he went out.

Dan turned his attention again to what was on the table. Beside the portfolio was a slim, bound file entitled *Bureau of Marine Accident Investigation—Fatal accident on board a UK registered trawling vessel*. It was the BMAI report Dan had been unable to obtain. There was also a safety report produced by Chesterton Fisheries. He left them where they were. John Wainwright had told him all he needed to know for now about his father's accident.

Now he focused on the portfolio. He reached out to touch it. He felt it. It was real. He slid the portfolio round to find how it opened. Finding the tab, he gingerly unzipped it. He gently lifted the cover up and back, resting it on the table to reveal the contents.

81

Inside there was a group of loose papers, of varying sizes. Each piece of work was individually separated by a wisp of tissue paper. As he looked at the collection, Dan thought how like an ancient treasure it was, that had been carefully stored away for posterity. Or a body that had been meticulously wrapped and prepared for burial, in contrast to his father's own watery grave. John hadn't just obtained a portfolio cover to protect Dan's father's papers. The way these things had been so tenderly preserved was an act of sacred trust.

Dan started to examine each piece of work, one after the other. He turned the pages over in his fingers, feeling their texture, scrutinising and pondering their contents.

There were photos. Some of them had been taken outside, presumably when the carcass was first brought on board. Others were taken inside, presumably in the galley. The carcass had been photographed from most angles, giving a good idea of how it looked in the flesh. It was white. Some parts had already started to decompose, revealing red muscles underneath. One photo showed the carcass stretched out, full length on the deck. Another showed the left side of the animal with its front flipper. A third photo had the carcass winched up above the deck, so that the long neck drooped over away from the body, in line with its front flippers.

There was a diagram that his father had drawn up. It showed the basic anatomy of the animal and was of the animal's skel-etal structure. Dan thought it looked rather like the plesiosaur model he had seen at the museum. Skull, neck, spine, and tail, as well as the large paddle-like flippers, were all detailed. There were measurements of the different parts of the carcass, too. Overall, it appeared to be about three metres long, divided fairly evenly between neck, body and tail. The flippers, or pectoral fins, also measuring about a metre in length, were either side of the neck where it joined the body and similarly either side of the tail base.

There were tests. His father had felt the paddle-like flippers, which were still reasonably intact, and had noted that he could feel the phalanges, that is, phalanx bones, inside. He also recorded the fact that he'd taken several samples in the hope that they would be analysed later.

And finally, there were his father's notes. Dan had never seen his dad's writing before. He knew the notes weren't personal, only for scientific purposes, but he chose to imagine that his father was writing them directly to him. He drew a deep breath as he began to read:

Having conducted a thorough examination and analysis of the carcass, it is, in my opinion, a plesiosaur-type mammal, presumably juvenile, considering its size. Reasons for this conclusion are as follows:

1. *The presence of flippers, or pectoral fins, two anterior and two posterior, all four of similar size. These flippers contain phalanges (bony fingers) which would be expected in the flipper of a mammal, rather than the cartilaginous fin rays that stiffen the fin of a shark.*
2. *The absence of a dorsal fin.*
3. *The surface of the body is whitish and covered with strong, dermal fibres which intersect each-other, as found in whales and other mammals. The fibres are not weak as found in fish.*
4. *There are thick, sticky, white, fat-like tissues on the back. This layer of fat is evidence that the carcass is almost certainly that of a mammal. Fat is not found in fish.*
5. *Reddish muscles can be seen running longitudinally beneath the white tissues, like those found in mammals and not occurring in fish.*

6. *The putrefactive smell is not like that of teleostean (ray-finned bony) fish or sharks, but resembles that of marine animals. The smell of ammonia, which is absent, would be in keeping with a fish or shark carcass.*
7. *The head is hard, exposing the cranium, unlike that of a fish.*
8. *The nares (nose holes) are situated at the front end of what remains of the cranium, unlike those of a shark, for example, where they are situated in the lower surface of the skull…*

After reading for quite some time, Dan closed his eyes, resting his head in his hands for a moment. When he looked up, he was disorientated. The cluttered, organic cabin surroundings, with the morning sunlight streaming through the cabin window, had disappeared. They were replaced by cleansed melamine and stainless-steel surfaces. No windows. Everything was made bright by the fluorescent light overhead. There was silence apart from the low whir of a motor somewhere behind him. And he was aware of a strange smell.

Dan was at the end of a long table. He could see someone sitting at it, down the other end, on the left. They were bent forward, intent on what they were doing. At first, looking at the person in profile, Dan thought he was looking at himself. Same curly, dark hair and ruddy complexion. But then he spotted the shadow of stubble along the jaw and the smile lines etched above the tanned cheekbones. He realised the person was older than he, a young man.

Papers were spread along the counter behind the seated figure. Stretched out on the table in front of him were the remains of a large, marine animal. Flippers front and back hung down either side of the table. The long tail faced Dan. He couldn't see the head end. The stench was now quite strong.

The young man got up and moved around the carcass,

examining sides, flippers, tail. Dan knew he was watching his father. Dan wanted to speak, to reach out to him, but he was afraid that he might disturb whatever was making this experience, this vision, possible. He didn't want it to end.

His father sat down again, furiously scribbling notes. It was as if he knew he was operating against the clock. Time was short to capture everything he could about this special, mysterious creature.

Suddenly, the alarm began to sound. The young man looked up and then hurriedly gathered together the papers he had been working on, putting them in a pile at the end of the counter. He then took one last look at the carcass before he grabbed the life-jacket that was hanging on the back of the door and left.

Dan was back in John Wainwright's cabin. He was still clutch-ing a page of his father's notes. He looked down. The ink on the diagram had smudged. One of his tears had fallen on it. Even though the galley vision of his father had dispersed, he still felt close to him in that place. He remained sitting there, very still, holding on to that remnant sense of closeness.

Eventually though, the sound of gulls crying outside brought him out of his reverie. Slowly and carefully, he put everything back in the portfolio the way he had found it.

CHAPTER NINETEEN

Dan found John working down by the slipway. The gulls reeled around their heads, making a racket.

"Mackerel close by," shouted John, pointing to the birds, "they'll pass soon."

He finished coiling the rope he'd been using and stowed it in the boat. The gulls did indeed move on out over the water, fewer and fewer of their calls being carried back on the sea breeze.

John leant back against the nearest boat and looked at Dan with surprise.

"Not taking your dad's papers?"

It was Dan's turn to be surprised. It hadn't occurred to him to take them.

"No, I hadn't thought of doing that," he said.

It didn't seem right to move them – not yet at least.

"Thank you for keeping them so well all these years. It was wonderful to find them at last. And I may be biased, but he seemed to do a really thorough job, especially considering how little time he had and how much he had to improvise there on the *Tara Belle*."

John nodded.

"You can be proud of your dad. He was a real gent and a true scientist. Really generous, too. And he loved everything about the natural world, especially the sea, and was always curious to find out more. It would have been a real crime if his work had been lost. And it didn't seem fair that he was discredited posthumously, with no opportunity to defend himself. I didn't know who I was saving his papers for, I just knew I had to take them for safekeeping."

John leant forward with a twinkle in his eye and said, "It didn't occur to me that one day his son would come walking into my yard looking for them."

He took out a cigarette paper and started to fill it with tobacco.

"You could try to get them published, you know," he said nonchalantly, still looking down at what he was doing. "I might be able to help you with contacts. Times have moved on. Water under the bridge and all that. It could be argued that a discovery like that belongs to the people of the world. At the very least, it would give those so-called experts a run for their money."

Dan turned the idea over in his mind. It would be very sat-isfying to publicly vindicate his father. A fitting tribute. But then something occurred to him.

"What about the Vested Interests? Wouldn't they just squash it all again?"

"Maybe. It's possible they would. It would be understandable if you didn't think it was worth the effort."

Dan thought about it again. He realised the most important thing was that *he* now knew the truth about the last day of his father's life. Did it matter what the world thought? Even if it did, was he really in a position to change anything, with or without John's help?

Maybe one day, when I'm older, he thought. *Who knows what the future will bring?* He realised that the future now looked far more hopeful. The bleak shadow over his life had dissipated.

"I'll think about it–keep it in mind," he said.

"Can't say fairer than that," said John.

Dan looked around the boatyard. He marvelled how it had seemed so foreboding only a short while ago and how threatening John had appeared at first. Now the place seemed positively welcoming.

"I have to tell you something," he said, wanting to come clean. "I have been here before."

"I know," said John. "I remember."

"Sorry."

"That's okay. I'd prefer you didn't visit like that again."

"No way! Never again!"

After a moment's silence, Dan asked, "Do you mind still keeping the papers here for now? I could come and see them again, yes?"

John lit his cigarette and smiled.

"You can come and see them whenever you want," he said, warmly. "They'll be waiting right here for you."

Dan's heart leapt. He wasn't used to things being so easy, so accommodating. He smiled.

"Thank you. Thank you for everything."

"It's an honour and a pleasure," John said, graciously.

Dan grinned even more broadly.

"I'd better be going, now. I have some chores to do for my grandmother."

"Well, we can't keep the lovely Eleanor waiting now, can we?" said John. "Off you go."

Dan headed for the gate.

"See you again soon," he called over his shoulder.

Deep in thought, Dan wheeled his bike along the promenade for some time. When he came to himself, he found that he was far past the turn off to the shopping centre he was supposed to be going to. In fact, he wasn't far now from the east end pontoon where Peter and Naomi kept their boat.

I need to tell them what's happened, Dan thought. *Maybe they're out sailing today.*

He hurried on towards the pontoon. When he got there, he

peeked into the shed. It always looked like it was locked, but when the boat was out, Peter left the door on the latch. The shed was empty.

Leaning his bike against the promenade wall, Dan sat beside it, looking out to sea. At first, he was looking for signs of Peter and Naomi in their boat. There was nothing as far as the eye could see. But as he continued to scan the waves, he recognised afresh the breath-taking magnificence of the ocean; the kind of beauty and magnificence he had tried to capture in his painting. He loved the sound of the waves as they broke on the shore, the whisper as they receded. He loved the wild force of the wind against his skin, through his hair. But he'd never dared to respond to the challenging call of the mighty sea, beckoning him out into its vast greatness. It had always been a foe, the one that had taken his father.

But now he knew that the sea hadn't caused his father's demise but had provided a final resting place for him. It was not the sea's fault that his father was no longer with him. Maybe, in time, the sea could be his friend.

Around the eastern head, a little sailing boat appeared. Dan knew it was Peter and Naomi. He made his way down the pontoon and stood there, waiting. Naomi had started to wave. The boat scudded briskly towards the pontoon, finally passing him and tacking round to come alongside.

"I saw you all the way from the head," called Naomi.

Peter was smiling but said nothing.

"I've got some news," said Dan. "I wanted to come and tell you. To tell you both."

"That's great," said Naomi, stepping onto the pontoon and starting to tie the boat up. "You can tell us over lunch. I'm famished!"

But Dan was looking at Peter.

"Hello," he said. He knew he had quite a bridge to mend with his friend.

Peter looked up at him.

"Hello," he replied cautiously, and then, almost automatically, "Want to come out for a spin?"

Dan stood there for a moment. He realised that everything had changed. He didn't have to repeat the same old ritual he and Peter had practised all these years. He was free.

"Yeah," he said, "I'd like to do that."

Peter looked surprised but pleased. Naomi started excitedly hopping from one foot to the other.

"Here, have my jacket," she said.

It didn't really fit, but somehow Dan managed to squeeze himself into it.

"Jump on board, over there," pointed Peter.

Dan gingerly stepped into the boat, instinctively moving to the middle to sit down.

"Take hold of that rope," said Peter. "That's for the jib. I'll tell you when to clip it in."

The mainsail started to flap as Peter steered the boat around. Dan felt the pull on the boat as the wind caught the sail and filled it. It was an odd sensation that made him feel nervous, but exhilarated, all at the same time.

"We've got good wind today," said Peter, as the boat started to move away from the pontoon. "Where to, Cap'n?"

Dan looked up to the top of the mast and then out across the water to the horizon.

"To where the sun sinks into the sea," he said, extravagantly, "And plesiosaurs still play, to this very day."

"Right you are, Cap'n," laughed Peter. "Setting course now. Due west it is!"

Dan felt an expectant thrill as the boat started to glide through the waves, ushering them out into the open sea.